The CHRISTMAS ADVENTURE OF SPACE ELF SAM

by AUDREY WOOD

illustrated by BRUCE ROBERT WOOD

THE BLUE SKY PRESS

An Imprint of Scholastic Inc. · New York

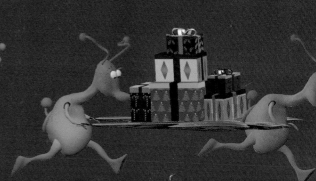

For James M. Carey, co-founder of Books of Wonder
— A.W.

For Don Wood, my surfing partner, my mentor, and my father
— B.R.W.

THE BLUE SKY PRESS

Text copyright © 1998 by Audrey Wood
Illustrations copyright © 1998 by Bruce Robert Wood
Art direction by Don Wood

For information regarding permission, please write to: Permissions Department,
The Blue Sky Press, an imprint of Scholastic Inc.,
555 Broadway, New York, New York 10012.
The Blue Sky Press is a registered trademark of Scholastic Inc.

Library of Congress catalog card number: 97-43718
ISBN 0-590-03143-0

10 9 8 7 6 5 4 3 2 1   8 9/9 0/0 01 02 03

Printed in Singapore   46
First printing, October 1998

The illustrations in this book were created digitally, powered
by Silicon Graphics, Alias/Wavefront 3-D imaging software, and Amazon 3-D Paint,
assisted by Adobe Photoshop and various MetaCreations tools on the Macintosh.
Iris prints by In·Color, Santa Barbara, California
Display type created by Jim Lebadd
Color separations were made by Bright Arts, Ltd., Singapore.
Printed and bound by Tien Wah Press, Singapore
Production supervision by Jessica Allan
Book design by Don Wood and Kathleen Westray

STORYTELLER'S NOTE

When pioneering families from Earth
began to settle on distant planets in the galaxy,
Santa Claus had a problem. He needed to deliver presents
to every child who lived in the space colonies, but he couldn't
fly his sleigh in outer space. So Santa opened the Space Elf Christmas
Academy. At the Academy, elves built fast spaceships and were trained
to deliver presents to all the families living on the far-flung colonies.
This is the story of Space Elf Sam and his Christmas adventure.

SPACE ELF SAM

GRADUATED FROM SPACE SCHOOL
WITH FLYING HONORS, BUT NOT IN TIME
to sign up for his first Christmas mission.
Sam was practicing a low-orbit cruise
around the moon when he received an
emergency call from Santa Claus.

"A bag of Christmas letters just arrived
from the children at the new space colony
on Alpha One," Santa explained. "There
are only three days until Christmas, and
the rest of the elf fleet left long ago.
These children must have their presents."

"Don't worry, Santa," the elf said. "I'm
on my way! Over and out."

When Sam arrived at the North Pole, he loaded Santa's presents aboard his ship. "The children on Alpha One are far from home," Santa said as he handed the elf a cup of hot chocolate. "It's up to you to get their Christmas presents there on time." "You can count on me, Santa," Sam said with a salute. And then he added:

"I didn't win this gold star on my belt for nothing! I'm the fastest pilot on the force."

Santa smiled at the proud young elf. Then he placed his own hat on Sam's head.

"Ho-ho-ho," he laughed. "Remember the Christmas spirit, Space Elf Sam!"

The elf blasted off into the sky, ready to succeed on his first mission.

Sam zoomed past planets and through an asteroid storm, singing "Jingle Bells" all the way. When an exploding star sent shock waves through the galaxy, Sam kept his ship so steady, he didn't spill a single drop of his hot chocolate. Then Space Elf Sam decided to take a shortcut. *I'll get there a day faster,* he thought. *Santa chose the right elf for the job.*

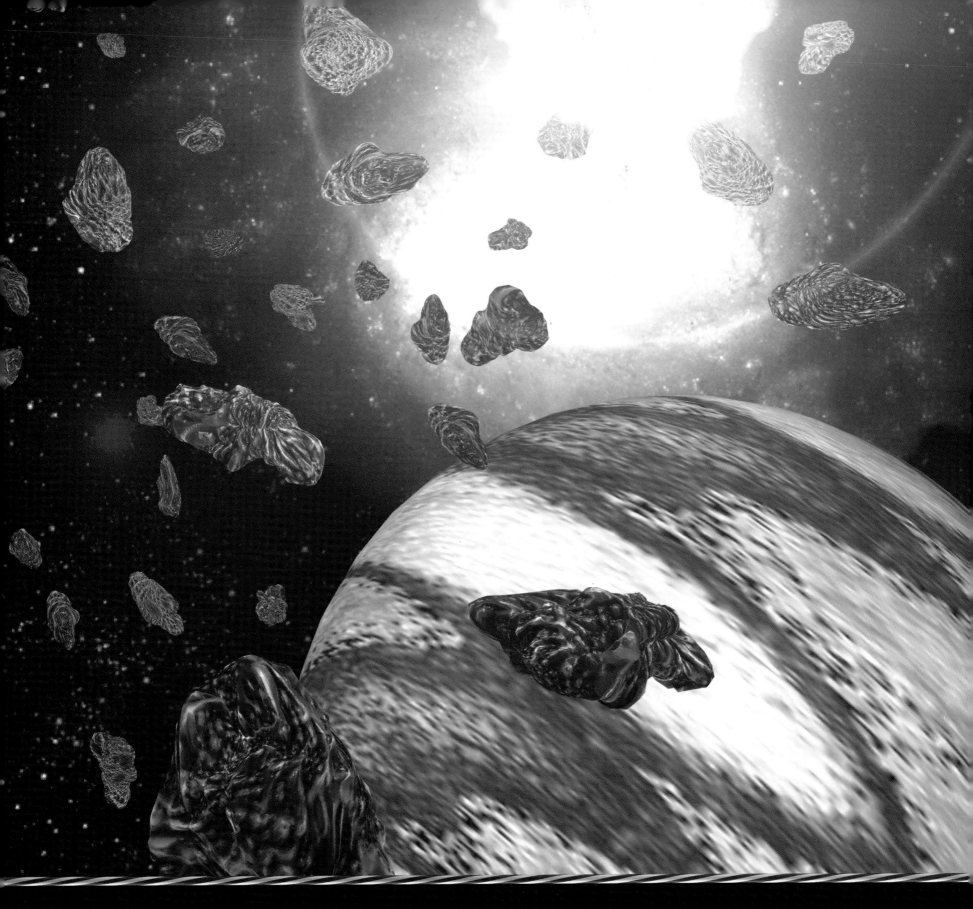

He pointed his ship at a giant hydrogen cloud and dove straight in. Everything was fine until Sam's spaceship popped out of the cloud. He tried to avoid a small comet, but it struck his spaceship, smashing the main thruster. Sam would have to crash-land on the unexplored planet of Gom.

As the ship skidded to a stop, the hatch flew open, scattering Christmas presents onto the ground. Sam climbed down to check the damage. He was in a strange world with ragged mountains and two suns. Little green aliens were everywhere!

"I'm Space Elf Sam from the planet Earth," he said in his bravest voice. "Take me to your leader!" Without answering, the Gommers grabbed Santa's presents and hurried away. "Stop!" Sam shouted.

Sam chased
the aliens down
into the ground.
He followed them
to a dark cell where
they were stacking
Santa's presents.

"Wait in the waiting
room," an alien said.

Sam entered the cell,
and a barred door slammed
shut, locking him inside.

"I'm trapped!" Sam cried. He checked his space watch. "Impossible!" he
exclaimed. "It's Christmas Eve! I must have blacked out when I crashed. I've lost an
entire day. Let me go!" he shouted, shaking the bars. "I have to repair my ship.

Presents aren't the most important part of Christmas, he thought. *But the children on Alpha One will be disappointed if there are no gifts beneath their trees.*

As the three moons of Gom cast an eerie light through the high window of Sam's cell, a tear trickled down the elf's cheek.

"Santa Claus!" he cried out in despair. "I have failed my first Christmas mission!"

The night passed quickly. Both suns were rising when the aliens opened the door. Once again, the Gommers gathered up the presents, and Sam followed them deeper into the ground. At last they came to a dark chamber where a King and Queen sat upon their thrones.

"What is this?" the Queen asked, holding up a present.

"It's a Christmas gift," Sam said.

"How does it work?" the King asked, sniffing a present.

"Well," Sam explained, "something special is inside. It's supposed to be opened on Christmas morning."

"When is Christmas morning?" the Royals asked.

Sam checked his space watch. "Right now," he said, "and it's very important that I deliver these presents to the children on Alpha One. I must put the gifts under their Christmas trees."

"What are Christmas trees?" the King wanted to know.

"Christmas trees grow up from the ground," Sam said, trying to be polite. "They have branches that stick out from tall trunks. Now I must go and repair my ship."

"No!" said the Queen. "Now you must follow us."

Space Elf Sam followed the Gommers outside and over a bumpy hill.

"Teebles! Teebles!" the Gommers shouted.

"We have Christmas trees, too," the Queen said, pointing to a strange creature.

When a Teeble leaned over and made a purring sound, Sam reached out and petted it.

"On my planet," he said, "part of the fun of Christmas is choosing just the right tree."

"We will choose," the Queen said.
After checking each Teeble, the Gommers found the one they liked best.
"Now our Christmas tree is ready," the King announced.
"Well, not exactly," Space Elf Sam admitted. "It isn't a true Christmas tree unless it has pretty things hanging on it, and colored lights that twinkle."
"Come!" the Queen commanded.
Popping out of the ground, the Teeble hopped behind on its one foot.

Before long, they entered a narrow canyon where colorful creatures dangled by their tails.

"Zogs are pretty things," the Queen said. "They will hang on our Teeble."

A multi-colored Zog licked Sam on his nose. "Tweep! Tweep!" the creature squeaked.

The elf laughed out loud in spite of himself. Soon he was helping the Gommers gather Zogs of every color.

With their arms full of Zogs, the Gommers led Sam into a foggy swamp.
Long, rubbery vines with oblong pods snaked along the banks.

"Winky-Winks!" the Gommers cheered, and the pods lit up in bright colors.
"By golly, you have twinkling lights!" Sam exclaimed.

When they returned to the throne room, the King asked, "What is next, Space Elf Sam? Tell us now!"

"Now we decorate your Teeble with Winky-Winks and Zogs," Sam said. "But the Winky-Winks must go on first. And don't forget to make it look good from all sides."

At last they were finished. The Teeble was purring happily, the Zogs were squeaking sweetly, and the Winky-Winks were lighting up the dark chamber with sparkling colors.

Everyone was in a festive mood, especially the little Princess.

"Your Christmas Teeble needs one more touch," Sam said. Taking the gold star off his belt, he held up the Princess and let her place it on the tip-top of the Teeble.

"Can we open presents now?" the Princess asked.

Space Elf Sam didn't know what to do. How could he give away presents that belonged to the children on Alpha One?

But it was Christmas, so. . . .Sam handed a present to the Princess.
Quickly she tore off the bow and ripped open the paper. Then she held
it up. Everyone's eyes opened wide.

It was a teddy bear. The Princess burst into tears.
The other little Gommers began crying, too.
"Are all of your presents so scary?"
the Queen asked. Suddenly
Space Elf Sam understood.

Gommers didn't know what to do with Earth presents. Taking off Santa's hat, he used it to wipe the tears from the little Princess's cheeks.

Then he looked at the hat in his hand, and he thought about Santa's words: "Remember the Christmas spirit."

"Don't cry!" he said to the Princess. "I know what to do. Each of you must find gifts for your family and friends— things that you know they will truly like."

The Gommers agreed and hurried away.

Before long, they returned, carrying unusual presents of every shape and size, each one wrapped and decorated. "We made name tags, too," the Queen said proudly. While the Royals read the names, Sam passed out the presents. Everyone was excited. The Queen could hardly wait for the Princess to open her gift.

"A doppleviper!" the Princess exclaimed with joy, hugging it to her chest.
"This present-giving is fun!" the Queen whispered to Sam.
After all the gifts were unwrapped, the King announced,
"Space Elf Sam gets a present, too. . . ."

Slowly a platform rose up from a deep pit. There stood Sam's spaceship, with nine shiny thrusters attached to the front.

"Your ship is ready for travel to Alpha One," the Queen said. "Their children should have Christmas presents, too."

Sam looked at his space watch. He couldn't believe how fast time had flown. "Why, it's already night!" he exclaimed. "Christmas is over. The children on Alpha One are asleep."

"But that is not true," the Queen explained. "Because we have two suns, time goes twice as fast on Gom. It's still yesterday on Alpha One. Hurry! The colony is not far away."

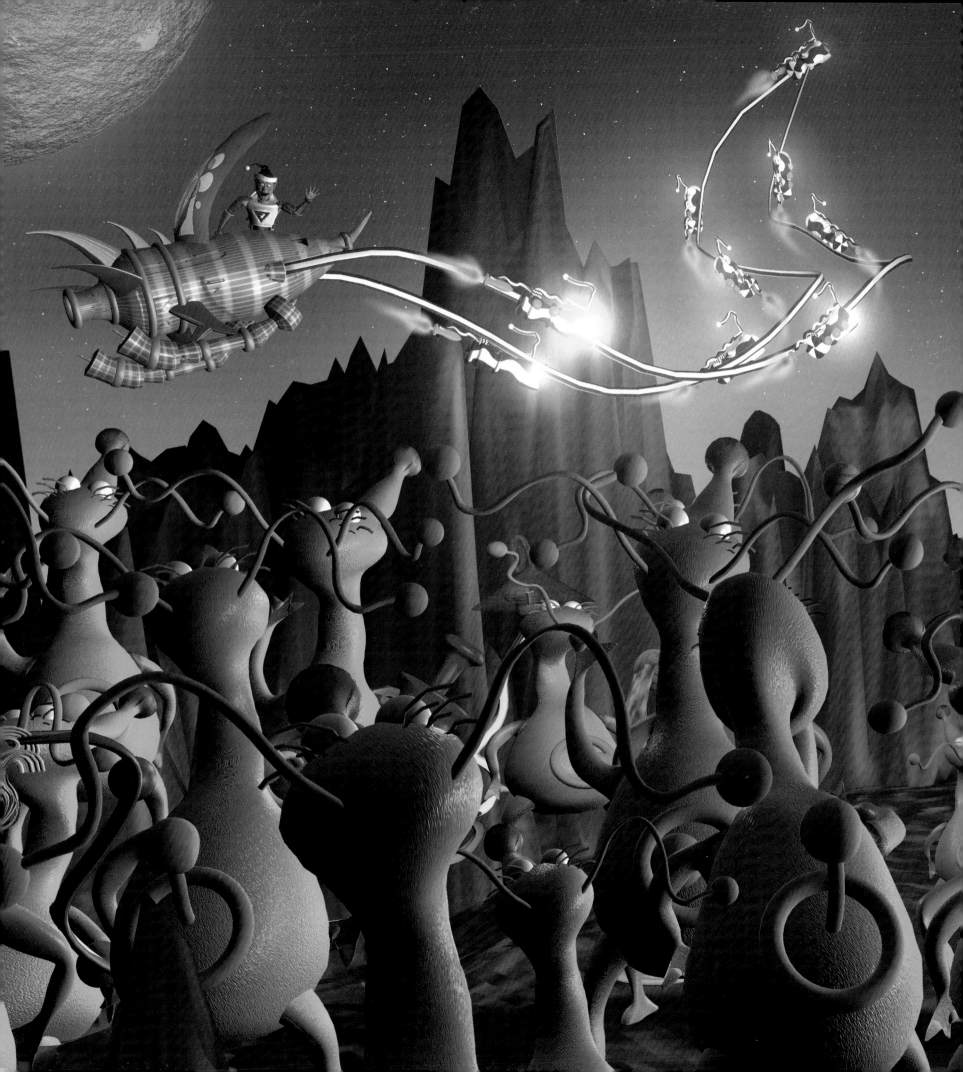

"Merry Christmas to all!" Space Elf Sam called to the Gommers
as the shiny thrusters pulled his spaceship across the sky.
The next morning, all of the children on Alpha
One had presents beneath their trees.
And since that time, all of the
Gommers on Gom have had
a Christmas, too. . . .

.but their Santa Claus looks
a bit different from ours,

and they get to celebrate it
twice as often.